Crabs

Heather Hammonds

Contents

Crabs

Crabs are animals that live on land
and in water.

There are many kinds of crabs.
There are little crabs and big crabs.

Crabs have ten legs.
They have claws on their two front legs.

claws

legs

legs

shell

Crabs do not have a **backbone**.
They have a very hard shell
on the outside of their bodies.

The shell helps keep their soft bodies safe.

Where Crabs Live

Some crabs live in the sea.
They live under rocks and in seaweed.

Crabs live on sand and in rock pools
at the beach, too.

Other crabs live in rivers and lakes.
They hunt for food in the water.

There are crabs that live on land, too.
They dig holes in soft ground.
The holes are called **burrows**.

What Crabs Eat

Crabs eat many kinds of food.
Sea crabs eat little sea animals
and sea plants.

The Blue Swimmer Crab
likes to eat little fish and shellfish.

Land crabs like to eat insects,
worms and other little animals.
They eat fruit, leaves and plants, too.

The Red Crab likes to eat seeds from water plants.

Baby Crabs

Baby crabs come from eggs.
The mother crab lays lots of eggs.
She carries the eggs on her shell
until they hatch in the water.

The baby crabs stay in the water
for about a month, while they grow.

Crabs that live on land
walk down to the sea,
so their eggs can hatch in water.

The baby land crabs stay in the sea
until they grow bigger.

Then they crawl out of the sea
and onto the land.

When Crabs Grow

When crabs grow bigger,
their hard shell does not grow, too.

They must grow a new shell
and leave the old one behind.

This is called **moulting**.

These Giant Spider Crabs are moulting.
Their new shells are soft.
Their new, clean shells slowly go hard.

The crabs hide until their shells are hard.
They stay safe from bigger sea animals.

Little and Big Crabs

Some crabs are so tiny that they are hard to see. This little Pea Crab lives inside a **shellfish**.

The crab eats the same small plants and animals as the shellfish.

It takes some of the food from the shellfish.

Other crabs are very big.
This Japanese Spider Crab lives
deep under the sea.
It has very long, thin legs.
It is the biggest crab in the world.

This crab eats sea plants and animals.

Clever Crabs!

Some crabs are very hard to see.
This helps keep them safe
from other sea animals.

This crab puts little seashells
and bits of sea plants onto its own shell.

Other sea animals cannot find it.

This crab looks like sand,
when it is daytime.

The crab can make its shell
look dark at night.
This helps it to hide.

It is fun to learn about crabs.
We can visit an **aquarium**
to find out more about them.

Glossary

aquarium   a place to visit and learn about lots of water animals

backbone   the hard part of the skeleton that is made up of many bones

burrows   holes in the ground made by animals

moulting   changing old shells, skin or hair for new ones

shellfish   water animals that live inside shells